Dedicated to my beautiful niece Mirabelle.
May your days be full of little and big miracles.

Published by: Ai Candi
Written and Illustrated by: Aileen Joy
Edited by: Laura Bracken
ISBN 978-0-692-88856-8

MIRACLE

Written and Illustrated by Aileen Joy

Meet a little fairy girl named Mira who was full of happiness and wonder.

She had a simple life. Every morning she would open her
small window to breathe the fresh air and fly with the playful birds.

Every night she looked up at the twinkling stars and sang with the musical crickets.

One day she sat on her favorite sunflower and wondered if there was more than her little home.

She wanted to see if she could find a miracle, and she flew away to explore the world!

The first place her wings took her was the big mountains.

She watched the white flakes fall like cotton balls covering everything!

All the flakes became piles of fluffy snow that she played in with joy!

It was a miracle that so many tiny snowflakes could cover
all of the mountains. She felt lucky to find a miracle on her first journey.

Next, she flew to the thick rainforest.

She swooped down on a giant leaf landing with a soft bounce.

She sat on a curly plant and watched the animals and bugs trotting across the forest.

She jumped up and twirled with the butterflies.
So many creatures living happy together was a miracle!

She glided out of the rainforest and dove into the ocean.

She was surrounded with bright sunshine and blue bubbles.

As she swam, she saw fish the color of rainbows and coral shaped like flowers.
There were mammals she never saw before like dolphins and seals!

She danced with her new friends.
It was a miracle that fish and mammals lived in the water, just as easily as she breathed air.
What would she find next?

When she poked her head above water, she found a sparkling sandy shore.

She swam to the shore and dried her wings in the warm air.

When she looked to the left, she saw a cave. Curious, she walked over to explore.

Inside there were little bats hanging from above.
One by one they started swooping into dark tunnels.
She was thrilled to see another miracle! The bats were able to find their way without light.

When she fluttered out of the cave it was night.
Bright fireflies and a full moon lighted her way.

She was sleepy and laid down on a puffy cloud.
She dreamt of all of the wonderful adventures so far.

The soft glow of the rising sun woke her up.

She opened her eyes and was surprised to see the miracle of the sun. The flowers bloomed and the morning animals started their day as the night animals went to sleep.

She soared across the sky and dove out of the clouds into the desert.

The land was dry but still growing and buzzing with life.
The cactus stood tall, and the reptiles were full of energy.

She soon felt a rain drop, followed by a few drops.
Then pouring rain! Suddenly, it stopped.

When the sun shined through the clouds, the desert brightened.
Animals came out of hiding to play in the water.
What a miracle the plants and animals could live in the dry desert for so long with no rain!

She loved her journeys. But she missed her bird and cricket friends. It was time to go home.

She found many miracles when she only wanted to find one.
She spread her wings and flew home.

When she got home, she was welcomed back with lots of hugs from her friends.
She discovered life can be both simple and full of miracles.
That is something she would never forget. Life itself is a miracle.

The end

Made in the USA
Columbia, SC
21 March 2019